The Bridge to Love

by

Alexa Aston

DRAGONBLADE
PUBLISHING, INC.

Dragonblade Publishing, Inc. is an imprint of Kathryn Le Veque Novels, Inc.
P.O. Box 23
Moreno Valley, CA 92556
ceo@dragonbladepublishing.com

Produced in the United States of America

First Edition September 2022
Print Edition

ARE YOU SIGNED UP FOR DRAGONBLADE'S BLOG?

You'll get the latest news and information on exclusive giveaways, exclusive excerpts, coming releases, sales, free books, cover reveals and more.

Check out our complete list of authors, too!

No spam, no junk. That's a promise!

Sign Up Here

www.dragonbladepublishing.com

Dearest Reader;

Thank you for your support of a small press. At Dragonblade Publishing, we strive to bring you the highest quality Historical Romance from some of the best authors in the business. Without your support, there is no 'us', so we sincerely hope you adore these stories and find some new favorite authors along the way.

Happy Reading!

CEO, Dragonblade Publishing

Additional Dragonblade books by Author Alexa Aston

Second Sons of London Series
Educated By The Earl
Debating With The Duke
Empowered By The Earl
Made for the Marquess
Dubious about the Duke

Dukes Done Wrong Series
Discouraging the Duke
Deflecting the Duke
Disrupting the Duke
Delighting the Duke
Destiny with a Duke

Dukes of Distinction Series
Duke of Renown
Duke of Charm
Duke of Disrepute
Duke of Arrogance
Duke of Honor

The St. Clairs Series
Devoted to the Duke
Midnight with the Marquess
Embracing the Earl
Defending the Duke
Suddenly a St. Clair
Starlight Night
The Twelve Days of Love (Novella)

Soldiers & Soulmates Series
To Heal an Earl
To Tame a Rogue
To Trust a Duke
To Save a Love
To Win a Widow
Yuletide at Gillingham (Novella)

The Lyon's Den Connected World
The Lyon's Lady Love

King's Cousins Series
The Pawn
The Heir
The Bastard

Medieval Runaway Wives
Song of the Heart
A Promise of Tomorrow
Destined for Love

Knights of Honor Series
Word of Honor
Marked by Honor
Code of Honor
Journey to Honor
Heart of Honor
Bold in Honor
Love and Honor
Gift of Honor
Path to Honor
Return to Honor

Pirates of Britannia Series
God of the Seas

De Wolfe Pack: The Series
Rise of de Wolfe

The de Wolfes of Esterley Castle
Diana
Derek
Thea

Also from Alexa Aston
The Bridge to Love

Prologue

LADY ANNE OF Glanville stood at the edge of the forest beside the old oak tree. She looked across the way, her gaze on the wooden bridge spanning the Medway River, the link between her father's property and that of Lord Windthorst of Windsong. Elric had told her to meet him here early, before morning mass began, because he had something very important to discuss with her. She spied movement on the other side and her heart sped up when Elric appeared.

Anne loved Elric with all her heart.

She couldn't remember a time when she hadn't known the handsome man who now began to cross the bridge to her side of the river. Two years older than she was, Elric had recently turned eighteen. He had fostered at Lord Morran's over the years, coming home only infrequently, but always making certain that he saw her when he returned to Windsong. She had watched him grow from a young, sturdy boy into the man that now ventured across the bridge, tall and broad-shouldered, with sparking blue eyes and thick, golden hair.

He spied her in the darkness and hurried toward her.

Reaching her, he took her hand and said, "It seems years since I last saw you, Anne." His eyes roamed her face as if he had asked her a question and awaited some kind of answer.

"I was glad to receive your message," she told him. "It is good to

1

see you, Elric. It always is."

Suddenly, he seized her shoulders, his eyes dark.

"I have something I must ask you," he said solemnly.

When he didn't speak, Anne asked nervously, "What do you wish of me?"

Elric said, "I wish for you to be my wife, Anne."

He bent, pressing his lips to hers for the very first time. They were warm and soft as they brushed against her own.

Her heart sang as she wrapped her arms about his waist.

The sweet kiss went on, warming her blood, stirring something unknown within her. Her childhood dreams were now coming true.

Elric broke the kiss, gazing down upon her now with a confident smile. "I want us to wed at once," he shared.

His determined words gave her pause, as if something stood in their way. "Why? What is wrong? What are you not telling me?"

Anger flushed his face as he said, "Father wishes for me to wed Lord Bronwyn's daughter. He wants a union between our two families," Elric explained. "The king favors Lord Bronwyn. Father hopes if I wed the earl's eldest daughter that our family will bask in that favor, as well."

"We cannot go against your father's wishes," Anne said dully, hurt filling her as the brief happiness had been snatched away. "I am a dutiful daughter and you have always been a dutiful son."

"He doesn't understand what I hold dear," Elric said. "I have loved you from the time we were children, Anne. I want to go on loving you throughout time."

"But how can you go against your father?" she asked. "If we wed, he would hate you—and he would certainly hate me."

"He will accept what is," Elric predicted. "I promise you that, Anne. I have already spoken to our priest, Father Michael. He knows my heart and how I feel about you. He is willing to help us. The question is, can you wed me under such circumstances?"

Anne swallowed, her thoughts swirling. She turned away from Elric, needing time to think, but knowing she didn't have that luxury. Her eyes turned to the tree trunk in front of her. The massive oak had stood here for many years. A set of initials were carved into it.

Her parents' initials.

They had been a love match and her mother had brought Anne to this tree from the time she could walk, pointing out what her father had scratched into the wood. Though her mother had died three years ago, she still lived in Anne's heart—and that of her father's. Lord Glanville had sworn never to remarry, wanting to remain faithful to the only woman he ever loved.

Anne possessed that kind of love for Elric. She would have her father's support in this endeavor. It would be difficult since Lord Windthorst had already chosen a bride for his son but Anne promised herself to be the best wife she could be to Elric and hoped that would win over his father.

She turned and faced her true love and saw the worry that filled his face.

Taking his hands in hers, she said, "I will wed you anywhere. In any place. At any time. I love you, Elric. I always have. I always will."

He beamed at her, the doubt falling from his face. "We will meet at midnight," he informed her. "Father Michael says we must have a witness to the marriage."

Anne frowned. "Who could we tell about this?"

"I have decided to ask Bickford to observe our union."

Anne did not like Elric's cousin. He was three years older than Elric and had come to live with the de Bergville family after his father's death over ten years ago. Bickford was far too arrogant for her taste. Knowing, though, that they required a witness for the ceremony, she could understand why Elric wanted to ask his cousin. Elric was an only son and family meant a great deal to him. It made sense to invite Bickford to act as their witness.

"When will you tell him of our plans?" she asked.

"After we sup this evening in the great hall. Bickford is in charge of the night patrols around Windsong. If need be as we leave the castle's gates, we can use the excuse that he wants to make a personal sweep about the estate. No one will question him."

Elric framed Anne's face in his large hands and said, "I will count the minutes until we can be together."

He lowered his mouth to hers again and the kiss brought her reassurance.

Breaking the kiss, he smiled down upon her. He took her hand in his, entwining their fingers, and pointed to the oak tree.

"I have always enjoyed the story of your father carving these initials into this tree. I want to do something similar."

As the sun began to break along the horizon, Elric led Anne to the center of the bridge, where he stopped.

"Just as many people will see your parents' initials on that tree over the decades to come, I also want others to see tangible evidence of our love."

He released her hand and pulled a blade from his boot.

Anne watched as Elric carved a heart into the handrail, a warm glow filling her. Then he carved his own initials into the wood.

"We will wed at this spot at midnight," he proclaimed. "And once we have been joined as man and wife, I will add your initials here. It will be a spot we bring our children to over the years and tell them our love story."

This time, it was Anne who wanted a kiss. She gripped Elric's tunic and pulled his mouth down to hers. Their lips joined together, just as their bodies would after they were pronounced as one in the eyes of God.

She pulled away, gazing steadily at Elric and said, "I love you."

Her beloved smoothed her hair. "I love you, too, my sweetling. Until tonight."

They parted, each walking in the opposite direction of the other across the wooden bridge. When Anne reached her side, she turned, seeing that Elric had also paused. She blew him a kiss and he pretended to catch it and tuck it inside his tunic.

Anne made her way back through the woods to her home. She hurried toward the chapel for morning mass, which was about to begin. Peace blanketed her.

When dawn broke tomorrow morning, she would be a married woman.

ANNE SLIPPED FROM her bed and donned her boots. She had called for a bath earlier, pouring in some lavender oil. Elric had once told her every time he caught the scent of lavender, he thought of her. She had dressed in a cotehardie of midnight blue, hoping the dark color would help her blend into the night. She prayed that she would find no one awake as she crept down the stairs and past the great hall, where dozens of people had bedded down for the night. No one stirred as she quietly opened the door to the keep and closed it behind her. She kept to the shadows, not wanting to alert any sentry to her movements as she made her way to the sally port.

Her father had showed her the secret door many years ago and she had gone through it numerous times. Her familiarity with the sally port helped as she made her way out it and kept close to the wall surrounding her father's castle.

The moon shone brightly but the evening was cloudy. Anne bided her time until the clouds crossed it, knowing that would aid in her escape. She raced across the open land in front of the castle and darted into the familiar woods.

She made her way quickly through the forest until she arrived at the oak tree. Pausing, she traced her fingers through the letters carved into the trunk, a smile on her face. She had made a love match as her parents had.

Turning, she watched with keen eyes, waiting for Elric to appear. Moments later, he did, the moonlight shining on his golden hair.

As Elric stepped onto the bridge, Anne moved toward it and did the same. They met in the middle. He clasped her hands and asked, "Are you ready to take this step, my love?"

"Never more ready," she declared, knowing she would walk through fire to be with this man.

She heard other footsteps on the bridge and looked to see the Windsong priest and Bickford heading toward them.

"I am Father Michael, Lady Anne."

"Thank you for assisting us, Father," she said earnestly.

"When Elric came to me and asked for this favor, I could not turn him down. He has told me many times over the years of his love for you. May God favor you and bless you with many children," the priest said.

Anne's eyes flicked to Bickford. She wanted to make an effort with him, knowing he was soon to be family.

"Thank you, Bickford, for being a part of this," she said.

Bickford nodded. "I was happy to hear of my cousin's secret plans." His mouth turned down as he added, "It will be difficult for my uncle to accept since he wished for a marriage with Lord Bronwyn's daughter but I am certain the two of you will bring him around."

Anne thought it churlish for Bickford to mention this but kept silent.

Father Michael asked them to join hands and face him. They did so and the ceremony began. As Elric pledged himself to her, she did the same, knowing how right their love was.

The priest called for a symbol of their love and devotion and Bickford produced a thin silver band, handing it to Elric. Elric slipped it on Anne's finger and then tenderly kissed her hand. His gesture moved her, tears misting her eyes.

The priest concluded the ceremony with a final prayer and Elric gave her a short, sweet kiss. Anne thought of how many kisses they would trade over the coming years.

Her new husband turned to Father Michael. "Thank you, Father."

"It was my pleasure," the priest replied, his eyes twinkling. "I will see the both of you at morning mass."

The holy man of God moved toward the Windsong side of the bridge. Anne waved goodbye to him and then turned her focus to Bickford.

"Thank you again for witnessing our marriage."

Bickford gave her an enigmatic smile. "I would see you safely back to Windsong."

"That isn't necessary," Elric said. He retrieved his blade. "I have something to do here before we leave. You may go ahead, Cousin."

Bickford shrugged. "If you insist." He stepped forward and without warning, brushed an unexpected kiss upon Anne's cheek. "Welcome to the family, my lady."

She shuddered involuntarily and heard his chuckle as he retreated from the bridge.

"Are you all right?" Elric asked, concerned.

She pushed aside the sudden uneasiness that filled her. "I am now that you are my husband."

His palm cupped her cheek. "I feel my love for you filling me, sweetling. Bubbling up and pouring from me." He kissed her. "Never has a man loved a woman as I love you, Anne. Our love will continue long after we are gone from this earth. May God let us always walk together, both here on earth and one day among the angels."

Raising his dagger, Elric etched an *A* inside the heart, next to his own initials. As he paused, she stepped closer and traced the letter with her finger.

"Now, shall I whittle a *G* for Anne of Glanville?" he mused. "You are no longer of Glanville. You are a de Bergville. I want it to be perfect, just as you are, my love. Our initials will be witness to our deep and abiding love. Years from now, others will walk across this bridge and wonder of the story behind the letters held within this heart. So, tell me—what shall I slice into the wood to bind us through all time?"

Her longing for him caused her to tug on his tunic, bringing his mouth down hard on hers. Elric's arms enveloped her and he kissed her deeply. A kiss of the promises he had made to her and all those to come in the years ahead. Desire flooded her, knowing they would soon join together physically. Hope filled her that a babe would result from their coupling tonight.

Suddenly, Elric was ripped from her arms. She saw a stranger wrap his beefy arm about Elric's neck. Bickford was there as well, his hand latching on to Elric's wrist, forcing the blade from Elric's hand. It hit the ground.

Anne thought to toss herself into the fray in order to give her husband a chance to escape but without warning, bands of steel encircled her, jerking her back, pinning her arms to her side. She struggled as Bickford stepped toward her, his smile now one of pure evil. The man holding her thrust her away from him and Anne stumbled. Bickford caught her and spun her about, one arm tightening about her waist as he yanked her to him. She opened her mouth to scream but his other hand covered her mouth, muffling her cry.

As she squirmed, trying to free herself, the man who had first held her joined the other stranger. Elric's eyes were wide with fright as he grappled with his captor. Anne could see her husband was losing the battle, his supply of air cut off.

"Loosen your grip, Castor," Bickford ordered. "I want him conscious. Help him, Fulk."

The one called Castor relaxed his hold, his arm still about Elric's neck. The other, Fulk, moved in, seizing Elric's flailing arms as he gasped for air.

"What do you want?" Elric wheezed.

But Anne knew. Fear filled her as Bickford's hand drifted up and tightened on her breast, squeezing it painfully. She shouted for him to stop but her words were stifled by his hand pressing against her mouth.

Elric fought to escape the two men holding him, anger sparking in his eyes. "Let her go. Don't touch her."

"Oh, but I do want to touch her, Cousin. I want the sweet Lady Anne—*and your title.*"

"What?" Elric croaked.

"I have always wanted to be the lord of Windsong," Bickford revealed. "Ever since I came. Only you stood in my way, Elric. You, the honorable, handsome, only son. If you are gone, I will be able to claim my heart's desire. Uncle's death. The title. The land. The wealth.

"And Lady Anne."

She twisted violently as she tried to escape Bickford's grasp.

"Do it," he commanded.

Without hesitation, Fulk grabbed a handful of Elric's golden curls and yanked his head back. He swiftly drew a dagger across her beloved's throat.

Elric's eyes widened in surprise and pain. He made an awful gurgling sound as Fulk released Elric's hair. As his head dropped to his chest, Castor stepped to the handrail. With Fulk's help, the two men tossed Elric into the river.

Bickford's hand dropped from Anne's mouth. A primal scream came from her, one of agony and lost hope. She broke away and rushed to the rail, looking frantically into the rushing waters and seeing nothing in the darkness below.

"You can now wed me, dearest Anne," Bickford said. "I always wanted you but you never glanced in my direction. It was always Elric."

"And it always will be, you cowardly bastard," she proclaimed. "Elric is my life and my only love."

With that, Anne, flung herself from the bridge.

She hit the cold river water, being swept downstream quickly. For a moment, she fought to keep her head above water. Then she forced her instinct to survive aside and surrendered to the water. She stopped trying to paddle. She felt herself being dragged down by the weight of her cotehardie. Opening her arms wide, she gave in to the water.

And drowned.

For what seemed a lifetime, Anne floated dreamily in the water, thoughts of kissing Elric keeping her happy. Then she found herself somehow standing. She looked about and immediately recognized the familiar surroundings.

She stood on the Glanbury side of the Medway River, next to the oak tree. Before her was the bridge.

The bridge to Elric.

She saw him on the Windsong side, looking wistfully at her. Eager to touch him—to kiss him—Anne ran the few feet to the bridge. She stepped onto it and then suddenly stopped.

It was as if she couldn't move. Her feet refused to lift. She took a few steps back with ease and then took a few more. Then she lifted her skirts and began to run.

Again, after only a few feet she stopped, as if some invisible barrier stood in her way. She looked at her feet, trying to understand what prevented her from continuing.

Raising her head, her gaze connected with Elric's. He stood sadly on the other side. He shook his head in defeat.

Anne tried again and again but could not break through, no matter how she availed herself.

Why couldn't she get to Elric?

And then she understood.

She was dead. So was Elric. And the bridge stood between them, keeping them apart.

For all time . . .

Chapter One

L ADY IRIS LANGLEY awoke, an emptiness spreading within her.
The Season was over and done.

Last night, she had danced the night away at a ball, the last social event until next April. While the evening had been enjoyable, Iris left without any offers of marriage. When this Season—her first—began, she held high hopes of finding a husband. Not just any husband.

The right husband.

Unfortunately, none of the many bachelors she had been introduced to met her requirements. Yes, she had many gentlemen call upon her over the last several months. But none of them stood out from the others. Her stepmother chastised her on a daily basis, accusing Iris of been too picky. Well, what was wrong with that? It was a husband she was considering, a man she would spend the rest of her life with. Of course she needed to be selective.

Her list included wanting a man who would treat her with respect and admire her as much for her brain as he did her beauty. Regrettably, almost ever suitor complimented her endlessly on her looks. Her dark, raven hair. Her deep, gray eyes. Her flawless complexion and beautiful smile. Though they weren't allowed to mention it, she had caught many of them perusing her hourglass figure, as well.

Not one gentleman seemed to wish to know anything about her, though. While she was inquisitive and asked others questions about themselves, her callers rarely—if ever—did the same. She could tell anyone who asked what Lord Dixon's favorite color was. That Lord Dutton preferred ham and Lord Brock enjoyed chicken. She knew Lord Crocker only went to see comedies at the theatre and that Lord Harris enjoyed gardening.

Not a single one of those titled gentlemen could provide one personal thing they had learned about her. She knew it—because she had finally asked each of them. They had all looked at her, perplexed, and then acted surprised when she lit into them, accusing them of merely courting her for her beauty and sizeable dowry.

Iris wanted to be seen for herself.

Crispin had seen her. He had known her likes and dislikes.

She had not seen her childhood friend in almost a decade. Once, they had been inseparable. Her father's estate, Glanbury, and Crispin's home, Windsong, almost adjoined. Only the Medway River separated their properties. For some reason, though he was four years older than Iris, Crispin had taken her under his wing when they were young. He taught her to skip rocks across a pond and fish in the river. He was the first to set her atop a pony and teach her about horses and how to ride. Iris had spent every summer day in Crispin's company and many other days of his school holidays with him.

But their lives changed. Crispin's first when his father, the Earl of Windthorst, died. Crispin was eleven and a second son so his older brother, Royston, inherited the title. Royston had just turned twenty-one. While their father had made time for both of his sons, Royston cared nothing for his younger brother, probably due to the age gap between them. Or simply because he was nasty. At least that's what Iris thought. Royston was selfish and manipulative and preferred to ignore Crispin when he returned from school. That actually gave Crispin and her more time together.

Then things changed again. And not for the better.

Iris' mother died in childbirth when she was ten. Lady Glanville had lost several babes over the years, never bringing any to term after Iris' birth. Finally, she had, though the boy was stillborn. Sometimes, Iris believed her mother died of a broken heart since she hadn't been able to provide her beloved husband with an heir.

Her father was inconsolable in the weeks after his wife's death. They were a love match, rare in Polite Society. She recalled the first time Mama had taken her walking through the woods. They had paused at an enormous oak tree. Mama had said it must have stood there for hundreds of years. She showed Iris where couples had carved their initials into the tree and had Iris find her parents' initials.

Mama had speculated on how many couples had etched their initials into the oak's trunk, a tribute to their love. She told Iris that one day she must have her sweetheart do the same so that she, too, could become part of the history of Glanbury.

Iris hadn't seen the lovers' tree since Mama's death. After a few months of grieving, Papa took her to London. Glanbury had been a happy place for him and he couldn't stand the thought of being there without his wife. Lord Glanville had them remain in town permanently so Iris hadn't seen Crispin again. Eventually, her father remarried a widow of great beauty.

And great cunning.

Iris hated her.

She had thought with Papa having wed again, they would spend the Season in town and then return to the country as most other families did. Iris missed country life. The clean air. The quiet. The peace. The new Lady Glanville, however, had no desire to live in a house where her predecessor had. She knew her husband had been in love with his first wife and seemed jealous of a dead woman.

Instead, the three of them had remained in town year-round. She watched as her father, who went into his second marriage with great hope, slowly saw those hopes shattered. The new Lady Glanville seemed to care little for her husband and nothing for her stepdaughter. As time passed, Iris heard the servants gossiping about the string of lovers their mistress took. She watched Papa grow more unhappy as time passed, caught in a trap of his own making.

Iris didn't want a marriage like that. She wanted one far different. One like Mama and Papa had experienced.

Perhaps she was looking for love.

Obviously, it had not come to her during her first Season. Now, London would empty out, a majority of the *ton* going to their country estates, while she would remain here, lonely and unsatisfied.

She thought again of the oak tree, filled with letters of lovers who had romantically placed their initials upon its trunk, each leaving their mark that spoke to their love for one another. She wanted a man who would understand why she wanted the same.

Would she ever find him?

Her thoughts turned to Crispin again. She used to daydream about him after she had left Kent. She wrote two, lengthy letters to him but he answered neither and she believed he had grown tired of her. Still, she had looked for him in the glittering ballrooms of London when she made her debut but never found him. After getting to know a few others who had recently made their come-outs with her, she'd discovered that Lord Windthorst, Crispin's brother, had died just before the Season began and that Crispin, a lieutenant serving in His Majesty's army, had come home to take up the mantle of earl as he mourned.

Perhaps knowing Crispin was in England, back at Windsong, is what had prevented Iris from forming an attachment to another man.

Because her heart told her she loved Crispin.

Would he even remember her? The little girl that worshipped him. And even if he did think of her fondly, how was she ever to see him again? Her stepmother refused to set foot upon Glanbury lands. Perhaps she could convince Papa that it was finally time to pay a visit to their country home.

Without Lady Glanville.

Now that Iris had a plan of action, she tossed aside the bedclothes and rang for her longtime maid. Rose soon arrived and helped her to dress for the day. She hoped to find her father at breakfast and was startled when she entered the breakfast room because her stepmother was also present. She rarely rose before noon, even when the Season wasn't in full swing.

As Iris took her place at the table, she felt anger hanging in the air. She looked to her father, the kindest and most gentle of men, and saw his face mottled red with rage. Quickly, she glanced to her stepmother and saw the fury in her eyes, knowing an explosion would soon take place. Lady Glanville was known for her volatile temper and the servants had always tread lightly, never knowing if or when they might be dismissed on the spot.

A footman placed a plate filled with toast points and a poached egg before Iris, her usual breakfast, while another footman brought her a cup of steaming tea. Both servants retreated to a corner, their expressions grim.

Deciding to venture into deep waters, Iris said, "Good morning, Papa. Good morning, Stepmama."

That was all it took for Lady Glanville to explode.

"How many times have I told you not to call me that?" she snapped. "I am not and never will be your mama. I am not old enough to be your mama. I have no desire to parent you in any way. You took none of my advice during the Season and that is why you now sit at this table with no offers of marriage. I cannot believe we are stuck with you for another year."

Before Iris could respond, her father slammed his fist down upon the table. "You will not speak to my daughter in that tone ever again!" He looked to the two footmen and their hovering butler and added, "Leave. Now."

With haste, all three servants exited the room.

Lady Glanville's eyes narrowed. "It must be something of importance you wish to speak to me about. Clever of you to have asked the servants to leave."

"I wish I could ask *you* to leave, Madam," Papa forced out, shocking Iris to her core.

"What is wrong, Papa?" she asked, knowing something was very wrong.

"What is wrong, Iris, is that I married this harridan. Or should I say slut?" His eyes flicked to his wife and back to Iris. "I was lonely for so many years after your mama's death. I finally thought it would be good for me—and you, since you would soon make your come-out—for us to have a woman's touch in the household again. How very wrong I was."

Papa rose to his feet and said to the countess, "You are a disgrace, Woman."

His wife shot to her feet, as well. "I am nothing of the sort, Glanville," she said icily. "I manage this household with aplomb. I am one of the leading ladies in the *ton* regarding fashion. You will apologize to me at once and perhaps I will consider forgiving you."

Her father scrambled from his place and, after a few strides, grabbed Lady Glanville by the shoulders, shaking her.

"You have betrayed me in every way possible," he said harshly. "Yes, I know about your parade of lovers. The thought sickens me. I am tired of you. Of everything about you."

Iris watched in horror as her stepmother slapped Papa, the red imprint of her palm staining his cheek.

"How dare you!" she roared. "I have done my best to be your countess and shepherd your daughter through her come-out Season. And this is how you repay me?"

She tried to pull away but his fingers tightened on her and he said, "I don't want to have anything to do with you, Madam. You disgust me. I rue the day I wed you and if I could, I would be rid of you."

"Then divorce me, Glanville," she hissed.

Iris gasped. No one in the *ton* petitioned for a divorce. It was a lengthy, expensive process—and it ruined the reputation of the couple involved in the proceedings. In turn, it would ruin her reputation, as well. Her hopes of ever marrying would be slim with such a scandal hanging over her family. Her gaze connected with her stepmother's and Iris saw the woman knew what she was thinking.

"If you divorce me, Glanville, it will ruin your precious daughter," Lady Glanville spat out.

Shock filled Papa's face and he released his wife, stepping back in horror. Then he looked at her with such contempt that Iris shuddered, wondering at the depth of his rage.

"Then we will lead separate lives from this moment on, Madam," he announced. "Iris and I will return today to Glanbury. You are to remain here in London."

"And when next Season comes?" Lady Glanville challenged. "What then?"

"Iris and I will return to this house. We will neither speak to you nor have anything to do with you. You will have the east wing to call your own but this is the last time I will ever address you, in private or public."

His gaze turned to Iris and he said, "We are going home."

Papa quit the room. Iris rose, having no appetite now. Her heart sang, however, knowing she would now return to her childhood home, to the place where she and Papa had been happy.

She rose and her stepmother said, "He thinks he has won. He hasn't. He will come crawling back to me. He needs me."

Iris shook her head. "You are a viper. Poison to everyone. Papa and I will be happier without you." She paused and then added, "And who is to say he won't take lovers himself? You have done so throughout your marriage, making no secret of it. You have not given him the expected heir. You have been more than a disappointment as a wife. You have been a disaster. I am only glad Papa has finally seen this and washed his hands of you."

Iris hurried upstairs, where she rang for Rose and told the servant they were departing London immediately and returning to Kent until the next Season.

Her maid's jaw fell. "Is that so, my lady?"

"Yes, Rose. We are finally going home."

Two hours later, she sat next to her father in their carriage. As they left London, she took his hand in hers.

"Thank you, Papa, for finally standing up to her."

"I don't know what I was thinking when I decided to wed her," he admitted. "She was a widow and had beauty and a maturity about her. I knew I could never love her but I did hope for an heir off her. Instead, all you and I received was heartache."

He squeezed her hand. "I am sorry I kept us from Glanbury for so long," he apologized. "I spent the happiest years of my life there with your mother. After her death, I could not see myself living there and had to escape. I knew my steward would mange things well for me and I thought being in town, you and I could create a new life for us. I have wronged you, Iris. I hope you can forgive me."

"There is nothing to forgive, Papa. We are going home, which is all I ever wanted."

Iris settled against the carriage cushion and gazed out the window, hoping by being away from Lady Glanville, both she and Papa could reclaim their lives and happiness.

She also planned to see Crispin. Something told her their meeting would determine her future.

Chapter Two

EXCITEMENT FILLED IRIS as they drew near Glanbury. Then she began giggling uncontrollably.

"What is it?" Papa asked.

Mirth filled her as she said, "I just realized that we have taken the carriage and horses. Lady Glanville has no transportation at all."

Her father erupted into laughter and Iris joined him, wiping tears from her eyes.

"I cannot see her walking anywhere, can you?" he asked. "She won't even cross the room to pick up a handkerchief and rings for a maid to bring it to her." He sighed. "Oh, it does feel good to laugh again. I don't remember the last time I did."

Papa squeezed her hand. "And it is good to see you smiling again, Iris. I don't recall you doing so the entire Season."

"That is because Lady Glanville keep thrusting undesirable gentlemen at me. She confirmed today that she wanted me to wed merely to get me out of the house."

He chuckled. "If she could have married *me* off to someone else, she would have done so."

Sadness filled Iris. "I am sorry you are saddled with her, Papa. I know divorce is out of the question."

"It is. It would ruin any chance you have of finding a husband. I won't do that to you."

"I wish you could find contentment, Papa."

He shrugged. "I found joy every day with your mother. I had hoped my new wife might provide me with companionship. I had just passed forty when I began courting her. I was lonely. Wanting an heir so that I could pass down my title. She pretended to be quite mad for me. It was only after we spoke our vows that she showed her true colors. She told me coupling was painful for her, both physically and emotionally. Even had her physician come and have a talk with me. He told me she had lost a child and was unable to have another."

Anger flared within her. "Then she should have told you of that before you wed. She must have known you wanted an heir."

"I should have clearly communicated that to her," he said regretfully. "If I knew she couldn't bear me a son, I never would have offered for her."

"Do you think she and the doctor lied to you?"

"I'm not certain," he replied. "I do know the act is not painful to her because she has had a stream of lovers in the two years we have been wed. I heard rumors of it. I would enter my club and the place would go silent. Finally, I hired a Bow Street Runner to get to the bottom of things. It may be true she cannot bear a child and that gives her the freedom to take as many lovers as she wishes without fear. I had planned to confront her about her behavior after meeting with the runner yesterday afternoon. I do apologize for things escalating as they did, especially in front of you. I would have kept this knowledge from you. That I felt young again because a woman a decade younger than me found me attractive. Now I know she merely wanted to secure her future. The runner told me that her lovers are all in their twenties. Young bucks she dallies with and then sends on their way. I was a such a fool."

Iris slipped her arm through his. "No, Papa, you were deceived by a wicked woman. Do not blame yourself for her evil ways."

"Perhaps she sensed that I could never give my full heart to her.

That it would always belong to your mother."

She sniffed. "That is no excuse for her abominable behavior. Please, let's forget about her for now. We are almost home. We'll be there for months." Iris sighed. "At least until next Season, I suppose."

"Do you not wish to go back to town for it?" he asked gently. "Were you that unhappy?"

"I don't know," she said honestly. "I missed the country dreadfully. And . . ." Her voice trailed off. She swallowed and then said, "I suppose none of the bachelors I met lived up to my image of the ideal gentleman. A man I would want to make my husband."

Papa looked at her sagely. "You mean none of them were Lord Windthorst."

Her cheeks heated. "I suppose I can keep nothing from you. Yes, in the back of mind, it has always been Crispin."

"You were close as children. I know his despicable brother is dead and that Crispin holds the title." He smiled. "Perhaps we should ask Lord Windthorst to dinner now that we are back at Glanbury."

"Could we, Papa?"

Hope filled Iris. She didn't know if Crispin would wish to continue their friendship from long ago, especially since he had never answered her letters. Still, they were adults now and neighbors. She wanted to see him. Talk with him. Only then would she know if something remained between them.

"I don't see why not. Of course, who knows how we will find Glanbury. We have been gone a good while."

The carriage slowed and turned into the lane that led up to the house. Iris' heart pounded and she gripped her father's hand tightly.

"We will find it is still home, Papa."

When they descended from the carriage, Mrs. Bennett greeted them.

"My stars! I had no idea you were coming, my lord. And Lady Iris." Tears filled the housekeeper's eyes. "Oh, my lady. How you have grown into a beauty. I haven't seen you since you were a girl of ten."

Iris embraced the housekeeper. "I have missed you and Glanbury, Mrs. Bennett. Papa and I are back. At least until next Season."

"Oh, Lady Iris, so much needs to be done. It's only me and one maid. And Cook, of course. We covered the furniture in sheets and let all the other servants go. It will take time to air your rooms and prepare the place for living again."

"Would it be easier if my daughter and I stayed at the village inn for a week or so, Mrs. Bennett?" asked Papa.

"That's an excellent idea, my lord. Staff will need to be hired. The place will need a thorough cleaning."

"Then we'll come every day," Papa declared. "Iris can help in hiring new servants and getting the household into order. I will spend my days with Mr. Tate, catching up on estate matters and visiting my tenants. He may be my steward but I want a hand in things again."

"Oh, it is ever so good to have you both back, my lord. But . . . what of Lady Glanville?"

Papa frowned and brusquely said, "She will reside in town."

"I see," the housekeeper said thoughtfully. "Well, come inside and we can begin to see what needs to be done."

"I think I will go into Aylesworth and secure rooms for us for the next week," Papa said. "Iris, you go with Mrs. Bennett. And we would like to invite Lord Windthorst to dinner a week from today."

The housekeeper nodded. "We will be in good shape by then, my lord."

Papa beamed. "Splendid—because two weeks from today, we will be holding a country ball. I want the neighborhood to know we are back."

"A ball, Papa? What an excellent idea."

Iris knew a country ball differed from most because not only would gentry from the neighborhood receive invitations but also the tenants at Glanbury and even residents in the local village. It would be the perfect way to reestablish former friendships and make new ones, as well as allow their tenants to see that Papa was truly committed to them.

Mrs. Bennett blew out a breath. "Well, I don't see why not. If we can hire a new staff and get the house back into order, hosting a country ball would thrill everyone."

"I will leave the details to you and Iris, Mrs. Bennett." Papa kissed Iris' cheek. "I'll go into Aylesworth now and put out the word that we are back and in need of servants, both in the house and the stables. We may have to send to London, however, in order to find ourselves a butler."

Mrs. Bennett cleared her throat. "Might I be so bold as to suggest my cousin, Lord Glanville? His name is Mr. Cutler and he recently lost his position. His employer closed his London townhouse due to poor health and will remain in the country. All the town servants were dismissed, including my cousin. I don't know if he's found another household yet but if he hasn't, I can recommend him."

"That is excellent news, Mrs. Bennett. Write to your cousin and have him come to Glanbury as soon as possible," Papa suggested. "You have served us for many years and I value your opinion. If you say Mr. Cutler is qualified, then the position is his."

"Thank you, my lord," said the grateful servant. "You will not be disappointed." Mrs. Bennett looked to Iris. "Shall we tour the house, my lady?"

"With pleasure," Iris said enthusiastically.

IRIS TOLD HER father goodnight and went upstairs to her bedchamber. She had chosen to keep the same one she had used as a girl. The past week had been a flurry of activity, with a bevy of servants being hired to get Glanbury back to a livable standard. She and Mrs. Bennett had been pleased with the results and asked all the new maids and footmen to remain. Cook had also been allowed to hire two scullery maids to assist her in preparing meals for Iris and her father and the new staff. More would come onboard in the coming weeks because her father wanted to fill the stables and hire a head groom and assistants to help care for the horses and vehicles. As of now, only their coachman from London handled the horses.

Mr. Cutler, their new butler, had arrived two days ago. Iris immediately saw the family resemblance between him and their housekeeper. True to her word, Mrs. Bennett's cousin proved to be a superb leader and eminently qualified to assume the reins over the household. Mr. Cutler had silver being polished and furniture moved within minutes of his arrival. He and Mrs. Bennett worked well together and Iris knew that Glanbury once more was in capable hands. Tomorrow, they would host Crispin for dinner and Mr. Cutler promised Iris that the country ball could easily take place the week after.

Because of his assurances and those of Mrs. Bennett, Iris had spent the better part of the day writing out invitations and having footmen deliver them to those in the community. Mrs. Bennett filled in a few of the gaps as to who still lived in the neighborhood, as well as in Aylesworth, and Iris would show Crispin her invitation list tomorrow evening to see if he could think of anyone else they would need to invite.

She looked forward to seeing him after so long a time apart. She told herself not to get her hopes up. Not to expect too much—actually, anything—from him. They were two people who had not seen one another in almost a decade. She knew they had both changed. Even matured.

But a part of her hoped that they could achieve the closeness they once had, as friends.

Or something more.

As she entered her bedchamber, ready to spend her first night back under Glanbury's roof, a sense of calm filled her. Being home after so many years had brought a peace of mind that she hadn't known during all her years in London.

And then she caught a whiff of lavender.

Iris closed the door and stepped into the room, something tugging at the back of her memory. She walked about, her brow furrowed. Then it occurred to her.

Her childhood playmate . . .

She had always smelled lavender when the young woman came to play with her. What was her name?

Iris now knew that Anne had been but a figment of her active imagination. She'd had no brothers or sisters and had merely invented someone to play dolls or pretend to take tea with her.

Anne.

Yes, that was her name. Anne. She had appeared to Iris when she was barely walking. For a long while, Iris thought Anne was real. She only came out when Iris was alone. She had welcomed Anne with open arms. She remembered sitting beside her as they turned the pages of a book. Anne watching her draw. Iris would prop up her dolls and she and Anne would play with them, even serving them tea with a child's set of dishes. Anne had even lain on the bed beside her when Iris took her naps. She recalled spending long hours talking to Anne. The young woman never spoke, only listened as Iris prattled on, talking enough for the both of them.

Gradually, over time, Anne had faded away.

Iris supposed it was because she grew older and didn't believe in imaginary playmates anymore. Or perhaps it was because she met Crispin and they began spending so much time together. Whatever the reason, Iris had no longer needed to have a make-believe friend—and so Anne had disappeared.

Still, every now and then, when Iris had entered her bedchamber, she could smell the faint scent of lavender, as if Anne continued to watch over her.

Why would she be smelling it now, so many years after childhood?

Feeling a bit unsettled, she rang for Rose. The sensible maid brokered no nonsense from anyone. Iris needed a good dose of the very sensible Rose.

The servant appeared. "You were busy today, my lady. All them invitations to write out. It took a fair amount of footmen to see them all delivered. Here, I've got your night rail already laid out on the bed. Let's get you into it for your first night back home. Oh, it's lovely to be at Glanbury again," Rose declared.

Her maid had the right effect on Iris, chattering away and dissipating the feelings of unease which had come over her. Rose had her sit at the dressing table and removed the pins from Iris' hair, brushing it out until it shone and then plaiting it into a single braid for sleep.

"Anything else you need tonight, my lady?"

"No. That will be all, Rose. Thank you."

Iris climbed into bed as the maid left the room and leaned over to blow out the candles before settling against the pillows. The sheer curtain panes allowed the moonlight to shine into the room. Iris never liked the damask curtains to be drawn at night because she was an early riser and liked morning light streaming into her room, gently awakening her.

She glanced about and then tried to shake off the feeling of being watched. She almost rose to close the curtains, which would plunge the room into darkness, but she was so weary. Instead, she closed her eyes, thinking of all she needed to accomplish tomorrow.

When she would finally see Crispin.

Iris knew it was a dream. Odd that she could be aware of that fact and yet not awake. In it, she opened her eyes and tossed back the bedclothes. She went to the window and glanced outside. The night was quiet. Still.

She turned and saw Anne standing there.

Iris looked at Anne with more mature eyes now. In her youth, she had thought Anne much older than she was. Now, she could see that Anne was no more than fifteen or sixteen. Her long, dark hair cascaded about her and Iris wondered why it hung loose. She had never really noticed what Anne wore but now she saw that it was as if Anne were dressed from another time, an earlier one, long before now.

"You came back," Anne said—though her lips did not move.

"We went away because Papa was sad that Mama died," Iris explained.

"I know. She was sad to leave here."

"Did you know Mama?"

Anne nodded. "I used to watch the two of you together. She loved having a little girl. And she was so happy with your father."

"They were a love match. Papa carved their initials into the lovers' tree."

Sorrow filled Anne's face.

"Did I say something wrong?" Iris asked, taking a few steps toward her friend.

"I loved once."

"Who was he, Anne?"

But Anne moved away, fading into the shadows.

Iris awoke with a start. She realized she was back in her bed and that she had only left it in the dream. The dream that had been of Anne.

Then she glanced to the foot of her bed.

Anne stood there, watching Iris, sadness enveloping her.

She gasped—and Anne dissolved into nothingness.

Chapter Three

S OMEHOW, IRIS MANAGED to fall asleep again though it had taken a good half-hour to do so. She awoke as the early morning light streamed into the room. Her window faced the east and so she always received the first light.

The vivid dream from last night came back to her.

Iris closed her eyes, drifting back to the dream again. She easily recalled Anne. What the young woman looked like and how she was dressed. What Anne had said.

That she had once loved someone.

Iris now believed that Anne was a ghost, not some figment of her childhood imagination. Anne had lived at Glanbury long ago.

The question was why her spirit still remained.

She wondered how many others had seen Anne over the years. She wanted to ask Papa if he had seen her but somehow she doubted it. It might be possible from what Anne had said that Mama had seen her. Or perhaps Anne had merely watched Iris and her mother. She felt no anger in Anne but sensed the immense unhappiness which filled the spirit. Was her melancholy caused by the man she loved? Had he not returned Anne's love? Had her parents kept Anne and her lover apart? Or had she died in childbirth?

Iris had so many questions. She was determined to discover Anne's identity.

"I will discover who you are, Anne, and why you are so unhappy," she vowed aloud.

Opening her eyes, for a moment she believed she saw Anne standing at the foot of the bed. Iris blinked and saw nothing was there.

Or at least nothing was there now.

"Anne," she said softly, "I want to help you. You stayed at Glanbury for a reason after your death. I must help you find a way to move on."

Determination filled her as she swung her legs from the bed and rang for Rose. She said nothing of seeing a ghost to her maid and would not even tell Papa. Still, she thought he might be able to help her uncover the identity of who Anne had been when she walked the earth.

At breakfast, Iris asked, "Do we have any records of Glanbury's ancestors, Papa? I know some families record births and deaths in their family Bible."

"What brought about this sudden interest?" he asked.

"I suppose as we prepared everything for us to live here again, it got me to thinking of all the ones who came before us."

"There is a book of some sorts. It is quite old. The first Earl of Glanville began it when he received the earldom. It lists births, marriages, and deaths. Would you like to see it?"

"I would," she said with enthusiasm, certain that she would learn something of Anne from this book.

They finished eating and Papa invited her to the library. Pulling the book from the shelf, he took it to a long table and opened it. Turning the pages carefully, he pointed.

"There is your name, Iris. Your mother's hand was much better than mine so she recorded your birth."

A lump swelled her throat and her fingertips touched where her name rested on the page. She noticed her mother had also recorded her marriage to Lord Glanville—and that her father had yet to make note of his second marriage to the current Lady Glanville, much less the death of his first wife.

"This is just what I was looking for, Papa," she said softly.

"Don't forget the old family cemetery," he reminded her. "Though no family members have been buried there for a good hundred years or more, it does contain your ancestors."

Iris had forgotten the space devoted to the graves of past residents of Glanbury since all Langleys were now buried in the church's graveyard in Aylesworth. Excitement rippled through her as she thought she might be able to find Anne's grave.

"I must leave you on your own," Papa said. "I am meeting again with Mr. Tate."

"Don't forget that we have a guest for dinner tonight," she reminded.

"I won't. I will be taking tea with Mr. Tate and one of our tenants this afternoon so I will see you and Lord Windthorst at dinner."

"Be in the drawing room at seven, Papa. We shall have drinks there and then go into dinner."

"That sounds lovely." He kissed her cheek. "You can tell us at dinner all about the preparations for the ball."

He left and she eagerly returned her attention to the book. Iris thought about what Anne wore and knew the clothing was nothing like the Georgian era or even the Stuarts and Tudors before. No, Anne had been haunting Glanbury for quite some time.

Gently closing the book, Iris opened it at its beginning and decided to work her way forward. The first entry was dated April of 1140 and noted that under the reign of Henry Beauclerc, Henry I of England, the earldom had been granted. It then listed the first Earl of Glanville, his name and date of birth, and his two marriages. Under each marriage appeared a list of children from that marriage, with their births, marriages, and dates of death recorded.

Iris began skimming through the book, carefully turning the thick, old parchment pages as she looked for Anne's name. She saw one but noted this Anne had died before her tenth birthday. Another Anne was listed several pages from that first entry but she, too, had died when she was five. Neither could possibly be her Anne.

Then she found an entry for a third Anne, born in 1264. She had two older siblings. One had become the next earl.

What Iris found incredibly odd, however, was that while Anne's date of birth had been recorded, no marriage or date of death had been entered. She continued studying each page until she reached Tudor times. Instinct told her that her Anne could not have lived during those times or later. That the ghost of Anne which Iris had seen over the years—and last night in her dream—was the Anne who was the only individual listed who did not reveal a date of marriage or death. Iris could understand if Anne wed and moved away why her date of death might have been a mystery. Yet throughout the book, even until now, all death dates were recorded. Well, except her own mother.

Why did this Anne have no mention of her death?

Puzzled, she returned the book to the shelf and decided to look in the graveyard. Once there, though, she found no answers. She discovered graves for Anne's two brothers, as well as her father and mother. Yet Anne had no grave of her own. It was as if she had disappeared and no one knew what had happened to her.

Had she run away with her lover? If so, why did her ghost haunt Glanbury? Had he made Anne unhappy? Or worse, had he abandoned her? Did she die in some hovel far from her home, only to have her spirit return to the place she had known happiness?

Iris had so many questions—and no answers.

She thought of the tree where lovers had placed their initials and hurried from the graveyard to the nearby forest. If she could find Anne's initials there, along with those of her lover, it might be a further clue in helping discover why Anne wasn't at peace.

Reaching the tree, Iris paused a moment. It loomed larger than any tree nearby, its trunk massive. She stepped closer and her fingers immediately found where her father had placed his initials and his bride's. Papa had done what no others had and also carved their wedding date below their initials. Iris had always thought that a thoughtful touch and longed for the day when her groom would do the same.

She searched the tree, looking high and low, circling about it until she had studied every mark placed upon it. Anne's initials weren't here. Sighing, she leaned against the tree.

And saw Anne.

The apparition was hard to see in the strong daylight but Iris knew it was her. Anne stood beside the ancient footbridge which crossed the Medway River, the link which she had crossed dozens of times on her way to meet Crispin. Iris had always been in a hurry and never once paused on the bridge itself.

Did this bridge have something to do with Anne?

Quickly, she hurried from the woods and toward the bridge. Anne watched Iris approach. As she drew near, she could see Anne was translucent. Iris could see the bridge behind Anne.

She reached the ghost and said, "I know you are a ghost, Anne. Does this bridge have anything to do with why you returned to Glanbury?"

Anne pointed as she slowly dissipated.

"Where, Anne?" demanded Iris. "Am I to cross the bridge?"

But the ghost had vanished. She would have to seek the answers on her own.

Iris stepped onto the bridge and walked across it slowly, looking at the planks of wood below her feet. The sides. The handrail. Where once she had scampered across it without any thought, this time, she moved slowly and deliberately. Her patience was rewarded when she reached the very center of the bridge.

Atop the handrail, someone had carved a heart. Within the heart were the initials *EdB* and below it an *A*.

Could this *A* be for Anne? And who was *EdB*?

Anne meant for Iris to find this clue. Though she hadn't the foggiest notion what it meant, Iris knew it might be the key to unlock why Anne roamed Glanbury hundreds of years after her death.

She would discuss this with Crispin tonight. He had always had a love for history and she seemed to remember he knew quite a bit about his ancestors. Maybe he could help her discover who *EdB* was.

And help Anne find peace.

IRIS NERVOUSLY LEFT her bedchamber. She wore one of her favorite gowns, a sprigged muslin with small cornflower blue hearts upon it. The hearts brought out the deep gray of her eyes. She'd had Rose roll her hair into a simple chignon, not wanting anything too fussy or formal for Crispin's visit.

She wondered what he looked like now. He had always been tall for his age, with thick, dark blond hair that lightened considerably during the summer months when they'd spent so much of their time outdoors. Those days now seemed a thousand years ago.

Tamping down her nerves, she went downstairs to the drawing room. Papa was already there.

And so was Crispin.

His blue eyes lit up when he caught sight of her and he moved across the room, taking her hands in his.

"It is good to see you, Iris."

His smile both warmed her—and made her belly flip-flop crazily. She had not worn gloves, seeing as how this was a casual evening at home with an old friend. Neither did he and his bare fingers clasping hers sent a heat up her arms, straight to her cheeks.

She pulled her hands from his, flustered, and curtseyed. "It is good to see you, Lord Windthorst."

He frowned. "There'll be none of that. You are Iris. I am Crispin. We are old, dear friends. My title cannot change that. Come, let us rejoin your father."

Iris allowed him to escort her across the room, where her father had plopped into his favorite chair. Crispin indicated the settee to Papa's right and she sat. He settled next to her, big and large and smelling absolutely wonderful.

Mr. Cutler appeared with a tray, offering them drinks. Iris declined after the others took theirs, fearing she needed to keep her wits about her tonight else she might blunder and reveal her true feelings to Crispin.

She admitted silently that she might have fooled herself all Season long, trying to be interested in other men, entertaining suitors who called upon her and doing her best to make a good impression at every social affair she attended.

When all along there had always been only one man for her.

Crispin.

She blinked a few times and focused on the conversation at hand. Papa and Crispin were discussing his time during the army. As she listened, the blood pounded in her ears, drowning out their talk. This would never do. She needed to get her feelings under control. She hadn't seen Crispin since she was ten and now she was nineteen. She needed to put aside her foolish crush.

But his thigh rested next to hers, causing a delicious warmth to continue to spread through her. His bergamot cologne beckoned her to lean closer and inhale him. Iris resisted that urge.

Barely.

She grit her teeth, willing herself to listen and quit daydreaming. Crispin was an earl now. He would want an elegant woman to become his countess. No matter how hard she had tried this past Season, Iris wasn't graceful, much less unemotional. Women of the *ton* looked blandly at everything and everyone, while she had a hard time keeping her emotions in check. Her heart might yearn for this man but she doubted he would ever see her as more than a girl, the tomboy she had once been. Though she now did fine needlepoint and could play the pianoforte remarkably well, he would look at her and remember her barefoot, climbing trees.

Their butler reappeared and announced that dinner was ready to be served.

Crispin turned to her. "You have been very quiet, Iris. I hope talk of my time at war didn't bore you."

"No, far from it, my lord. I was only surprised to hear that you had left school and went straight into the army without a stop at university."

His mouth tightened. "Royston held the purse strings. He believed a university education would have been wasted on me, especially since I was destined to go into the army anyway. He purchased my commission and I went off to war, wet behind the ears and most likely the greenest officer in His Majesty's army."

He offered her his arm. "May I escort you into dinner?"

"Of course."

They followed her father down the hall and into the small dining room. Iris had thought it more appropriate with only the three of them to dine here instead of at the table which seated a good thirty-six.

Crispin seated her and both men took their places, with Papa at the head of the small table and their guest to Papa's right. Iris was across from Crispin and hoped she would be able to eat without staring at him.

She relaxed as the first course arrived. Crispin had a way of putting everyone at ease and soon the three of them were laughing as old friends should. Two hours later, they adjourned to the library, where the men drank their port and Iris allowed herself a small glass of sherry.

After a few minutes, Papa rose and said, "It has been a long day and I wish to retire. Please don't think of leaving just yet," he told Crispin. "I know you and Iris are old friends and have much to catch up on."

"Goodnight, Lord Glanville. Thank you for the dinner invitation. And the one to your ball. It arrived this afternoon."

Papa smiled. "It may have been my idea to hold a country ball and reacquaint us with our neighbors but it is Iris who is seeing it come to fruition. All thanks should go to her. Goodnight."

Once her father was gone, Crispin turned to her. He took her hand and gazed deeply into her eyes.

"It is so very good to see you again, Iris. I feared I might never do so."

"You could have seen me if you had attended the Season."

He frowned. "Once I received word of Royston's death, I sold out and returned to Windsong. I knew it would be in disarray because everything my brother touched became a mess. I needed to sort out the estate instead of gallivanting off to London."

Crispin continued to hold her hand and Iris' mouth grew dry.

"I worried every day and night that word would arrive of your impending marriage. I heard in the village that it was your first Season. I was positive some gallant bachelor would sweep you off your feet and I would never see you again."

"That didn't happen," she said softly, her belly now doing somersaults.

"No. It didn't." His gaze held hers. "Why is that, Iris? Why would a beautiful woman such as you not take a husband?"

She licked her lips nervously. "Because no man interested me." She paused and added, "Because no one was *you*, Crispin."

There. She'd said it. He now knew. He might laugh a bit. Tease her some.

Instead, his fingers tightened on hers. His free hand cradled her cheek.

"I have never forgotten you, Iris. I have thought about you every day for the last decade. When I awoke. When I fell asleep at night. When I marched into the heat of battle."

"You did?" she squeaked.

"I did," he assured her. "I know we were merely children but I always saw our friendship blossoming when we grew older. Becoming . . . more."

She bit her lip. "But . . . I wrote to you, Crispin. You did not answer my letters. I thought you wanted nothing more to do with me."

Anger sparked in his eyes. "I never received any letter from you. I can only assume that Royston kept them from me." His thumb stroked her cheek. "I would have written you back. I would have written you every day, Iris. I almost did write to you before I left for war. So much time had passed, though. I thought you had forgotten me."

Her hand clasped his wrist. "I never forgot you," she said fiercely. "You were my world."

"And you were mine." He looked at her tenderly. "May I kiss you, Iris?"

"I may die if you don't," she told him.

Crispin chuckled. "Always honest. Always truthful."

"Not something valued much in Polite Society, I'm afraid," she said ruefully.

"We don't need the *ton*. Because we have each other."

He framed her face with his hands and his mouth touched hers. Slowly, he brushed his lips against hers, bringing goosebumps to her arms and causing her pulse to flutter wildly.

She had never been kissed. Every time a suitor had tried to do so, Iris had turned her head or stepped away. Somehow, she had been saving herself for this moment.

This perfect moment.

Crispin's fingers slid to her throat, his thumb rubbing where her pulse beat wildly. His hands moved to her shoulders, holding her steady as he increased the pressure on her lips. A sense of urgency overwhelmed her and her hands grasped his coat. Iris gripped it tightly as Crispin's hands lovingly moved up and down her back before he drew her to him. Her hands slid up his hard, muscled chest and pushed into his hair, so soft and silky.

Then his tongue glided slowly along her bottom lip, bringing a frisson of desire. She opened to him and his tongue swept inside her mouth. Mating with hers. Exploring. Teasing. Tormenting.

The kiss went on, becoming more demanding. More possessive. Iris gave herself over to Crispin, knowing he would always protect her.

Finally, he broke the kiss. They both panted, their foreheads resting against one another's, hearts racing. Crispin's hands cradled her cheeks.

"I love you, Iris. I have my entire life. Marry me. Please say you will be mine."

"Yes," she replied breathlessly. "I love you, Crispin. You are my everything."

Iris caught the scent of lavender as Crispin kissed her tenderly.

Chapter Four

IRIS SNUGGLED AGAINST Crispin's side. No, not Crispin's side.
Her betrothed's side.

"I still can't believe we are engaged," she said softly, the wonder of knowing she would spend the rest of her life by Crispin's side still so new.

He tilted her chin up for a sweet, lingering kiss.

"Do you think Papa knew of our feelings and that is why he left us alone tonight?"

Crispin chuckled. "Your father has always been most astute. He also is a man who was very much in love with his wife."

"Papa remarried two years ago," she revealed. "A widow ten years my senior."

"He what?"

Iris nodded. "I was surprised but knew he was lonely. He told me he sought companionship and had hopes of an heir."

"Where is Lady Glanville?"

She snorted. "We left her in London. She is a terribly wicked woman, Crispin. She deceived Papa and did not tell him she could no longer have children. Supposedly, she lost a babe during her first marriage and is never able to have another one."

"That is very sad for Lord Glanville, I'm sure."

"What's even worse is that once she had the protection of Papa's name, she betrayed her marriage vows repeatedly." Iris sensed her cheeks flushing but added, "She has taken lovers. Several of them."

"That's terrible!" Crispin proclaimed.

"Apparently, it is an open secret in Polite Society. Papa confronted her about it just before we left town last week. He broke all ties with her. They will now lead separate lives."

"That is why you returned to Glanbury?"

"Yes. Papa couldn't stand to be here after Mama passed. That is why we left so abruptly." Iris sighed. "I told you about this in my letters to you."

He smoothed her hair. "I am sorry I never received any of them. If Royston wasn't already dead, I'd have to kill him myself because he kept you from me."

He kissed the top of her head and entwined their fingers together. "I am sorry we were separated for all those years."

"Would you have come to London for me?" she asked.

"I've thought about it ever since I returned. Royston left things a bloody mess, though. My first duty was to my tenants." He smiled. "But yes, I had plans to seek you out if no word came of you wedding some gentleman."

"I am so happy, Crispin."

"I am, too, love. When would you like us to marry?"

"Do we have to wait long?" she asked. "I don't want to waste any further time."

"Then we will have the banns read come Sunday. That gives you three weeks to plan our wedding."

"It won't take much planning," she assured him. "I already have a gown I can wear. That is what usually takes the longest. I would like to keep it simple. A bit of greenery to decorate the chapel. What about guests?"

"I bow to your wishes."

She thought a moment and then suggested, "Why don't we keep

the ceremony small and then open up the wedding breakfast to our tenants and the rest of the neighborhood?"

"I like that idea." Crispin dropped a sweet kiss on her lips.

"Do you smell that?" Iris asked, getting a faint whiff of lavender.

"What?" He sniffed the air. "Hmm. Lavender, perhaps?"

"Yes!" she cried. "So, you *can* smell it."

"I do." He leaned close and kissed her neck. "But you are not wearing any. Where is it coming from?"

"Don't think I've gone mad when I say this," she began. "But I believe it is our resident ghost."

Iris explained how Anne used to come to her when she was a child, playing with her when no one was around.

"By the time we met and became friends, she had already begun to come around less. Then as I spent time with you, she seemed to disappear. It was almost as if she knew you would watch over me and she no longer needed to. But . . . she is back."

"You have seen her? A ghost?"

"I believe so."

She detailed the dream she had and what Anne had revealed to her in it.

"When I awoke, I caught a glimpse of her. I promised to help her, Crispin."

He looked bewildered. "But what can we do?"

"She lingers because she is unhappy. We have to find out why— and help her leave."

Iris retrieved the family book and showed Crispin the entry.

"So, only her birth is listed. No marriage or death."

"That's correct. I combed through this book and she is the only person in it with incomplete information. I also went to the family plot of graves to look for her. I found her two brothers mentioned here in the graveyard, as well as her parents—but no Anne. I'd hoped to find a clue at the lovers' oak."

"You mean the tree with all the initials of couples carved into it?"

"Yes, that's the one. Crispin, I *saw* Anne there. She appeared to me again. She was so transparent, I could see through her. She indicated the bridge to me and so I searched it."

Eagerly, she explained the heart she had discovered, with *EdB* and *A* inscribed.

"I believe she is the *A*. If we could find out who *EdB* is, that might be the final piece that could solve this puzzle. I remembered how much you enjoyed history. Could you help me?"

"Of course." He stroked her cheek. "And I already know *EdB* must be one of my ancestors. I am Crispin Bergville—but the family name used to be de Bergville."

Iris clapped her hands. "So Anne was in love with a de Bergville. Do you know of any records your family kept?"

Excitement lit his face. "I know exactly where they are. I used to pull them out and study them as a boy. We will find who *EdB* is and hopefully use that information to help bring Anne to rest."

She threw her arms about him and kissed him with enthusiasm. "Oh, thank you, Crispin. For believing me. For wanting to help me."

Suddenly, the scent of lavender grew stronger and Iris gazed about the room.

"There," she whispered. "By the fire."

Anne stood there, a look of hope on her face.

"We will find out who your beloved was, Anne," Crispin told the specter. "And we will do our best to help you find solace."

The ghost smiled sadly at them as she slowly dissolved.

IRIS BOUNDED OUT of bed at first light and rang for Rose. As usual, her maid entered with a smile.

"Good morning, my lady. You see most happy today."

She couldn't help herself and burst out with, "I am going to wed Lord Windthorst!"

Iris twirled about the room and then collapsed onto the bed in laughter.

"Why, that's wonderful news, my lady. You two were always peas in a pod back when we spent all our time at Glanbury."

"Seeing him again last night made me understand why none of the gentlemen appealed to me this past Season. I love him, Rose, I truly do. And he loves me. We are going to be married!" she shouted. "But you mustn't tell anyone yet. I need to speak to Papa this morning."

"I'll be silent as the grave, my lady. You can count on me." Rose paused. "Will . . . will I go with you to Windsong?"

She leaped from the bed and threw her arms about the servant. "You better. I can't do anything without you, Rose."

Relief filled the maid's face. "That's wonderful, my lady. When is the wedding?"

Iris explained how the banns would be read tomorrow in church. "That means we will have three weeks to prepare."

"What are you going to wear? Might I suggest the light blue silk gown?"

She laughed merrily. "That is the very one I had in mind."

As Rose helped her to dress, they discussed how Iris should wear her hair and what should be served at the wedding breakfast.

"Lord Glanville will be so pleased," Rose noted. "And you won't have to put up with any more of Lady Glanville's meddling in your life."

"There is that." She smoothed her skirts. "I am off to breakfast with Papa. Once I have done so, I want the entire household to know." She twirled in a circle three times, laughing, and then exited her bedchamber.

Dashing into the breakfast room, Iris came to an abrupt stop. Crispin was seated at the table.

"What are you doing here?" she asked, moving toward him.

He rose and took her hands. "I wanted to do things properly, love. That meant speaking to your father before you did."

She beamed up at him. "I do love you, you know."

He bent and gave her a swift kiss.

Iris looked to her father. He had also risen and held out his arms. "Come here, my darling child."

She stepped into his embrace, relishing his warmth, knowing they had his support for their union.

Looking up at him, she asked, "You don't think it's too soon, do you?"

He chuckled. "It was years in the making, Iris. No, I am happy to see you so happy. Lord Windthorst will make for a fine husband. He has already told me just how much he loves you and how terribly he plans to spoil you."

She glanced to her fiancé. "Spoil me? Oh, I do like the sound of that."

Crispin seated her next to him and they spoke over breakfast about the upcoming wedding.

"I've already ridden into Aylesworth this morning to let the vicar know to begin the reading of the banns at tomorrow's service and that we will need his church in three weeks' time."

"Already?" she asked, laughing. "My, you must have gotten to the vicarage quite early."

Crispin grinned sheepishly. "I wanted to make certain there would be no delays. I hope you don't mind but I arranged for the wedding to be the Monday morning following the third calling of the banns."

She slipped her hand into his. "I think that is a perfect day for our wedding."

They finished eating and Iris told her father that she would be spending most of the day at Windsong.

"Ah, looking over your new home, I suppose," he said, looking a bit forlorn. "I will miss you, Daughter."

"You are welcomed anytime at Windsong, my lord," Crispin said. "No invitation is required. You are family. I have no father and I hope I may look upon you as one."

Papa took Crispin's hand and shook it. "I may never have a son of my blood but you will be the son of my heart."

His words moved Iris to tears.

"I am off. Mr. Tate has a dozen things for us to do today," Papa said. "Will I see you for dinner?"

Crispin replied, "I will make certain Iris is back by then, my lord."

Once Papa left, Crispin told her he had ridden over and asked if she would like to ride back.

"We don't have any horses for me to use," she lamented. "Only our carriage horses."

A wicked gleam came into his eyes. "Then I suppose you'll simply have to ride with me."

They went to the stables and Crispin mounted his horse, reaching down and taking her up in front of him. Iris liked how her fiancé wrapped his arm possessively about her waist and pulled her into his chest. Crispin directed his horse into the woods and had them pause at the lovers' oak.

"Shall we carve our initials into it now?" he asked.

This was a moment Iris had dreamed of her entire life, ever since her mother had showed her this tree.

"Yes," she said with enthusiasm.

Crispin helped her from the horse and pulled a blade from his boot. "Where would you like them?"

She showed him the spot next to her parents' initials and watched as he sliced through the wood. When he finished, she blew on it and then traced her fingers along the letters.

"This makes it very real," she said softly.

He kissed her in reply, a long, soul-searching kiss that had Iris hungering for more.

"Shall we?"

"Can you lead your horse across the bridge?" she asked. "I want you to see the initials resting there."

Crispin took the horse's reins in one hand and hers in his other and they stepped onto the bridge. At the halfway mark, Iris showed him the initials surrounded by the heart.

"Let us go see if we can locate this *EdB* in the family archives."

Leaving his mount at the stables, they entered the house and came across the butler.

"Soames, gather the servants in the foyer in ten minutes' time," Crispin instructed.

While they waited, he took her to the portrait gallery, showing Iris a picture of his parents. They looked utterly bored.

"We will have ours done, as well, except I believe our expressions will be markedly different from my parents' faces. They tolerated one another. Barely." He slipped his arms about her. "I intend for everyone to know we are a love match."

Crispin kissed her and Iris couldn't wait for them to truly become as one.

Leading her to the foyer, she saw it packed with servants. Apprehension filled her. Soon, she would be the mistress at Windsong and in charge of all of these people.

Crispin laced his fingers through hers and climbed a few of the steps so that they might be able to see all who had gathered.

"I wanted to let everyone know that Lady Iris has agreed to become my countess. We will be married in just over three weeks."

Cheers broke out, along with thunderous applause. She saw the nods of approval. Crispin moved to the bottom of the staircase and introduced every servant as they came by, giving them well wishes. Last to file by were Mr. and Mrs. Soames, the butler and housekeeper.

"We are delighted at the news, my lord," Soames said.

"I look forward to working with you, Lady Iris," Mrs. Soames said. "I know you will wish to make some changes."

She smiled at the housekeeper. "I hope you will advise me on any that I might want to make."

"Why don't you allow Mrs. Soames to give you a tour of the house?" Crispin suggested. "I will look through the family records while you do so then you can join me."

Iris was eager to see her new home. Though she had visited Windsong several times, it had been many years ago.

"I will see you in an hour or so, my lord," she said formally, eager not only to see her new home but to be behind closed doors so she could kiss Crispin again.

Chapter Five

ONCE IRIS JOINED Crispin again, she saw he had several open books scattered about a table.

"Have you found him?" she asked hopefully.

"I have. Thanks to you first finding Anne, I had a better idea of a starting point. Since she was born in 1264, I searched for de Bergville men who had been born between the years 1244 and 1270."

"Twenty years before her birth?" she asked, puzzled.

"It's not as unusual as you think. Why, women today are regularly wed to men their father's age. A twenty year gap between them wouldn't be uncommon. That's why I also extended my search a few years after her birth date, as well. During that time, I only found one son who had been born whose Christian name started with an *E*. Elric. Elric de Bergville. It has to be him."

Crispin led Iris to the open volumes, using his finger to skim down a page until he located what he wanted her to see.

"Look here. Elric de Bergville, born to Hrodwyn and Livith de Bergville. You can see Elric was the firstborn of three children and the only male. You can see where neither of his sisters survived childhood."

"1262. So he was two years older than Anne," she mused.

"Yes. With neighboring estates, I'm certain they would have known one another." He pointed back at the entry. "And look—no marriages indicated for him. What's even more significant? There is no recorded death."

"Just like Anne," Iris said, a chill running along her spine.

"Exactly. I looked through the entries for pages before and after Elric. Every person mentioned has both a birth and death date."

Iris began pacing about the room, trying to work things through in her mind. "Do you think they ran away together?"

"It's a thought but I don't see why they would have. Elric was obviously the heir to Windsong, being the only son born of the marriage. Why would he walk away from a title and property and most likely wealth?"

"It just doesn't make sense. They both disappeared from their family's histories. We have evidence of their love, thanks to Elric's etching their initials in the heart on the bridge." She paused. "What puzzles me is why he seemingly didn't finish? Why did he only carve an *A* for Anne and not complete the rest?"

"That is part of the mystery," Crispin said. "If we could find out why he didn't, it might help explain the reason why Anne still walks at Glanbury all these years later."

Crispin turned back to the book. "Elric's cousin, Bickford, became the next earl. From this record, it shows Bickford's father died when the boy was only ten. He must have come to live at Windsong if he didn't already. With Elric's disappearance—or death—Bickford assumed the title upon Hrodwyn's passing."

"What of the graves?" she asked. "We should look for Elric's stone just in case."

"Come, I'll take you now."

Crispin led her outside and they walked almost half a mile before they arrived at a small graveyard.

"This is where de Bergvilles were buried for many years. Like your family, we eventually began placing our dead in the church cemetery at Aylesworth."

They searched the graves. Iris found many of the headstones so worn that she could only make out a few numbers or letters. They did find both Hrodwyn and Livith's resting places, along with Bickford de Bergville. But no sign of Elric could be found.

"I should see you home now," Crispin told her. "You have had a full day."

They returned to the stables and, within twenty minutes, found themselves back at Glanbury. He escorted her to the front door.

"I'll keep at it," he promised. "You do the same. Between the two of us, we are bound to come up with an answer."

"I hope so," Iris replied, glancing around. Seeing no one, she pulled him down for a quick kiss. "Will I see you tomorrow?"

He beamed. "Tomorrow—and every day for the rest of our lives, love."

THE NEXT THREE weeks passed quickly. The country ball proved to be a rousing success and Iris and her father became reacquainted with many of their neighbors and tenants thanks to it. Since the banns had been read the Sunday before the ball, everyone was aware of her engagement to Crispin and they had spent a good portion of the evening receiving good wishes from all present.

Her father had allowed Crispin to address their guests during supper and her fiancé invited everyone in the room to attend their wedding breakfast. Because of the large number expected, the cooks at Windsong and Glanbury had been in constant communication, with both providing an equal portion of the wedding breakfast food.

Iris had spent a good deal of time at Windsong, overseeing a few changes she wished to make. She discussed all the redecorating with Mrs. Soames and found the housekeeper to have both good judgment and excellent taste. Working with Mrs. Soames in the years to come would be a delight.

Her only disappointment had been in being unable to learn what had happened to Anne and Elric. Iris was convinced the pair had been sweethearts and she had begun to suspect foul play, telling Crispin that would be the only reason for the couple's disappearance and why Anne seemed doomed to walk Glanbury forever. She blamed Bickford de Bergville, who had inherited the title of Earl of Windthorst, and believed somehow Bickford was responsible for Elric and Anne vanishing.

She longed to catch sight of Anne again but the ghost had made no more appearances to her. A few times, she had smelled a whiff of lavender and quickly studied her surroundings, seeking out Anne to no avail.

It was now the eve of her wedding and Iris made her way upstairs to her bedchamber for the last time. Tomorrow night she would be wed and sleeping in Crispin's bed. He'd told her there would be no separate sleeping arrangements. He wanted to fall asleep with her in his arms and awaken to her every morning. It delighted Iris that he felt that way and she felt her love grow for him.

Rose helped her disrobe and prepare for bed, brushing out Iris' hair and braiding it.

"Just think, my lady, tomorrow night we'll be under Windsong's roof," the servant said. "I've got you all packed. Your trunks will be delivered to Windsong first thing in the morning."

"Thank you for handling all that, Rose," she murmured, crawling into bed.

She lay awake for a while, hoping for a final glimpse of Anne. Finally, Iris sat up.

"I am leaving, Anne. I know you have seen me with Crispin. Tonight is my last night before I depart for Windsong. Please, help me understand how to bring you peace. I don't want you to walk the halls of Glanbury any longer. I want you happy. With Elric."

At the mention of Elric's name, the room flooded with the scent of lavender.

"Come to me again in my dreams, Anne," she pleaded. "Help me to help you."

With that, Iris rested her head against the pillow and feel into a deep slumber.

Once again, she knew it was a dream. It was night and she stood in the woods, near the old oak. Only one set of initials had been inscribed into its trunk. Iris watched as Anne came through the trees. Iris wanted to call out to her but found she couldn't speak.

Anne didn't acknowledge Iris' presence. She paused at the tree and traced her fingers along the letters before sweeping past Iris. Iris innately knew Anne had touched her parents' initials. They had been the first placed on the trunk, starting a tradition that had lasted over hundreds of years.

Then Iris watched Anne happily rush toward the bridge. A handsome young man with golden hair crossed from the Windsong side. The couple met in the middle and joined hands. It startled her how much the two resembled Crispin and her. She had never thought about it but she shared Anne's raven hair and gray eyes. Elric was tall and had an athletic build similar to Crispin.

Then a priest and another man appeared. She understood the man to be Bickford. The two joined the couple at the center of the bridge and Iris watched as they spoke their vows, tears in her eyes. Then the priest and Bickford left, while Elric and Anne remained. Even from this distance, she could see the love for one another shining in their eyes.

She moved to the edge of the bridge, wanting to hear what they said. They kissed and Elric said, "Never has a man loved a woman as I love you, Anne. Our love will continue long after we are gone from this earth. May God let us always walk together among the angels."

Tears blurred her eyes as she saw Elric take a dagger and make a mark within the heart. Anne's finger moved over it in wonder.

"Now, shall I whittle a G for Glanville? You are no longer a Glanville but a de Bergville. I want it to be perfect, just as you are my love. Our initials will be witness to our deep and abiding love. Years from now, others will walk

across this bridge and wonder of the story behind the letters held within this heart. So, tell me—what letter shall I slice into the wood to bind us through all time?"

Iris held her breath as the pair kissed again.

But the scene quickly changed. Chaos swirled. Suddenly, others were there, restraining Elric. Bickford had returned and held Anne captive. Iris tried to step onto the bridge, wanting to help, but it was as if she were frozen to the spot. Bile rose in her as she witnessed Elric's throat cut, his body hoisted over the handrail. It dropped into the raging waters of the Medway River.

Anne broke away and raced to the spot where Elric had disappeared. She and Bickford exchanged angry words—and then Anne threw herself from the bridge.

Iris stood in shock.

And then Anne suddenly stood next to her, her large gray eyes full of sadness. She reached out her hand, a wail piercing the night air. Iris looked and saw Elric standing on the Windsong side. He tried to take a step onto the bridge—and couldn't.

Understanding flooded Iris. The two lovers had not wanted to leave this earth without each other. They had returned, the bridge connecting them, and yet somehow keeping them apart. Their strong love had united them in death but something still bound them to this place.

Iris moved onto the bridge, walking slowly across it until she reached the middle. She glanced down and saw what Elric had etched onto the handrail.

And she knew now what must be done.

Iris awoke with a start. She saw Anne silently standing beside the bed.

"I understand, Anne. I will have Crispin help me. We will come to you once we are wed."

Anne reached out and placed a cold hand on Iris' cheek. Then she vanished.

Determination filled Iris as she rose. Today was not only her wedding day.

It was the day she would right the wrong done to Anne and Elric more than five hundred years ago.

She rang for Rose and, soon, the preparation began in earnest. Hot water was brought, along with a light meal for her to eat. She was bathed and dressed and her hair artfully arranged.

"You look lovely, my lady," Rose said, tears brimming in her eyes. "But there's one more thing to do."

Confused because she thought she already looked her best, Iris frowned as the maid withdrew something from her pocket and handed it to Iris.

She took the small box and opened it, her heart pounding as she saw what lay against the velvet.

A heart-shaped brooch composed of diamonds.

"Lord Windthorst gave it to me yesterday," Rose explained. "He said it was his wedding gift to you and you should wear it to the altar. That you would know what it meant."

Deep emotion flooded her and she said, "I do know." Her fingers trembled and she said, "Would you place it on me, Rose?"

The maid grinned. "With pleasure, my lady."

Once the brooch was attached to her gown, Iris looked into the mirror. "It's perfect," she whispered.

Papa waited for her in the foyer and watched as Iris descended the stairs. Tears filled his eyes as he took her hands in his.

"Your mother would have been so proud. I know she is watching over you." He squeezed her hands. "And she—and I—are so happy that you have made a love match, Iris."

Papa pulled her toward him and enveloped him in her arms. They held on to each other a long moment and then he released her.

Offering his arm, he said, "I believe we have a wedding to attend," his smile bright.

The drive to Aylesworth only took a few minutes and the carriage pulled up in front of the church. Papa climbed out and helped her down the steps. They moved to the church's doors.

He paused before they entered and said, "I hope you have more years with Crispin than I did your mother. Whatever comes, though, cherish each day you have with your husband."

"I will, Papa. I promise."

He nodded and their footman opened the door, allowing them to step inside the church. Iris' eyes immediately searched for Crispin. He stood at the altar next to the vicar, looking so tall and incredibly handsome. She floated down the aisle on Papa's arm, her heart swelling with love for this good man.

Crispin took her hands in his and raised them to his lips, brushing a tender kiss upon her knuckles.

"I know how to help Anne and Elric," she whispered. "But we must go to the bridge."

His eyebrows arched—and then he rewarded her with a brilliant smile.

"I always knew you were a clever girl."

The vicar cleared his throat loudly in disapproval, frowning at them. "Are you ready to proceed, my lord?"

"Yes, Vicar. More than ready."

As the clergyman opened his Bible and looked down to find his place, her groom flashed her a wicked grin.

Chapter Six

THE REST OF the ceremony progressed without a problem and, within the hour, Iris found herself wed to Crispin. He escorted her down the aisle and outside to the waiting carriage as the handful of guests cheered.

Once inside, he pulled her onto his lap for a long, delicious kiss that lasted all the way from the church to Windsong, where the wedding breakfast would take place.

As their carriage arrived, he broke the kiss. "You have figured out how to help our hapless lovers?"

Iris giggled. "My head is spinning from that kiss. But yes, I know what must be done. Let us attend to our guests and then we will make things right once again for Anne and Elric."

Crispin helped her from the carriage and they entered Windsong, which already felt like home to her. The breakfast was being held in the ballroom since so many were expected. They entered and a resounding applause broke out. Her new husband led her to a table for two in the center of the room and they took their seats.

Once the guests from their wedding arrived, Crispin signaled Soames and the butler soon had footmen delivering dishes to each table. They feasted upon several courses, getting up to mingle with those present between each course. Finally, a large cake was rolled in and Iris and her groom cut the first piece of it together.

By now, champagne had been distributed and Papa called for a toast, saying, "To my wonderful daughter and the man who has made her so happy. I give you Lord and Lady Windthorst."

"To Lord and Lady Windthorst!" the crowd echoed enthusiastically.

They made the rounds throughout the room and it took a good hour to speak with those they hadn't already. Once that was accomplished, they paused at the door leading from the ballroom. Crispin thanked everyone for coming and escorted Iris from the room, sweeping her into his arms and carrying her up the staircase to earl's suite.

He closed the door behind them and took her through a sitting room to the bedchamber, where he placed her gently upon the bed.

"I thought we could go to the bridge now," she began.

Her husband placed his index finger against her lips. "No. It will take forever for the guests to disperse. I'm sure they would question us if we passed among them and left to go to the woods." He began tracing her lips with his finger. "Besides, I can think of something to do to pass the time until we can slip into the woods unnoticed."

Heat flushed her cheeks. "You mean . . . you wish to couple now? It is still daylight!" she said, shocked at the idea.

"Oh, we will make love despite the hour of the day, love," he told her, his eyes darkening. "And in many places beyond this bed. We will couple before breakfast and after. In the stables and while beside the lake as we picnic. We will spend long, lazy afternoons together in this bed, the sun shining down on your beautiful body. Forget anything you have heard and lose any assumptions, Iris. Our lovemaking is for us and us alone."

She twined her arms about his neck. "Very well, my lord. Let this exploration begin."

Crispin undressed her slowly, kissing the newly-exposed skin as he did. Eventually, Iris wore not a stitch. Her husband flung off his own layers of clothing with abandon and captured her in his arms. Soon, he kissed her everywhere. Behind her ears and her knees. Along her nape down to the small of her back. Up her calves to her inner thighs.

And then her core.

Iris never knew such things existed as Crispin made love to her with his hands and lips and tongue. He pierced not only her throbbing core, brought to life by his sweet caresses, but her soul. And when his cock pushed inside her, they began a memorable dance of love, their bodies moving in time to one another, the pleasure immeasurable, the love hot and strong.

He collapsed atop her and then rolled to his side, still inside her as he kissed her thoroughly.

Breaking the kiss, he asked, "What do you think of marriage so far, Lady Windthorst?"

"I think being married suits us very well, my lord."

They lay cradled in one another's arms for several minutes and then Crispin released her. He brought a cloth and basin of water to the bed and tenderly ministered to her.

"Enough time has passed," he said. "We must go help our ghost. What do you have in mind?"

"First, we should get dressed," she teased. "Be sure to bring your blade again."

Crispin latched on to her waist and lifted her from the bed, pausing to kiss her before he released her.

"Shall I play lady's maid to you?" he asked. "You may return the favor and be my valet."

Iris giggled. "I shall look forward to it, my lord."

Once they were both dressed, she quickly braided her hair into a single plait. Crispin had pulled the pins from her hair and they were scattered everywhere. She hadn't the patience or the skill to try and duplicate Rose's handiwork.

Their fingers entwined, they slipped from the room and down the staircase, encountering only Mr. Soames.

"We are going for a walk, Soames," Crispin said crisply.

"Very good, my lord," the butler replied.

They left Windsong and made their way across the front lawn and toward the forested area. Iris recounted her dream to Crispin along the way.

"It doesn't sound like a dream to me."

"I agree," she said. "It was as if Anne made me a witness to what occurred."

"You were right to suspect foul play. I hate that I spring from Bickford."

She squeezed his hand. "Royston was more like Bickford. You would never have murdered someone in order to gain a title."

"I hate that Anne had to watch her beloved slain before her very eyes," Crispin said. "And that she drowned. That's a horrible death to endure."

"It would have been more horrible if she had lived and was forced to wed Bickford. Especially when her heart belonged to Elric."

As they drew near, Iris could hear the Medway River gushing. Soon, the bridge appeared and she directed Crispin to its middle section, where Elric had carved the heart.

"I forgot to tell you thank you for my brooch. It's perfect."

"It reminded me of Elric and Anne and their love," he told her. "From what you overheard, it seems they have a love that will never die." Pausing, he then asked, "So what am I to carve?"

"I believe that Anne will be reunited with Elric if you complete what should lie within the heart. Because they were already wed, use her married initials. Elric was interrupted before he could finish his task and leave a reminder to the world about their enduring love."

"All right," Crispin said.

He brought up his knife tip to the wood and stilled. Gooseflesh broke out along her arms as their gazes met.

Then Iris turned to her right and saw Anne standing on the Glanbury side of the bridge, her hand resting on the rail. Hope filled Anne's face. Iris glanced to her left and gasped.

Elric stood on the Windsong side. He, too, gripped the rail, eagerness on his face.

"We know how to reunite you," Iris called out. "Crispin and I wed today, just as you did so long ago. Today, you will come together in the afterlife and your spirits will no longer be bound to this place. The bridge which has kept you apart will now connect you once more."

She touched Crispin's back. "Go ahead."

"Help me," he said. "It should be the both of us doing this."

He took her hand and placed it atop his and then began moving the sharp tip back and forth against the wood. Iris felt chills ripple through her as they worked together.

The moment the final curve of the B was complete, the air about them changed. Crispin slipped his arm about her waist and they stepped back, remaining directly across from the heart. Iris watched as joy filled Anne's face and the ghost stepped onto the bridge and ran across it. She stopped in front of them.

Elric joined her, his smile full of love. He reached out and the ghosts joined hands, gazing deeply into one another's eyes. Iris felt the waves of love emanating from them.

Both spirits turned toward Crispin and her, so transparent that she could see straight through them.

Anne once again touched Iris' cheek in gratitude. Elric placed his hand on Crispin's shoulder. Instead of the cold she had felt from before, this time, warmth filled Iris at the touch.

Then the ghosts began to glow. Color filled their faces and rippled down their bodies. She saw Anne wore a gown of midnight blue and Elric's tunic was a dark hunter green. She thought she heard the words thank you though neither ghost spoke aloud.

The pair stepped away, their fingers going to the handrail where the heart lay. Elric smiled and embraced Anne, kissing her. For a moment, they looked as real as any humans. Then slowly, the vibrant colors grew fainter and fainter until the couple faded into nothingness.

"They are at rest now," she said knowingly. "Together. Forever."

"Just as we are," her husband said. "I hope to love you as long and as well as Elric has loved Anne."

Crispin kissed Iris tenderly.

Something told her they would one day meet Anne and Elric.

But not for a very long time . . .

About the Author

Award-winning and internationally bestselling author Alexa Aston's historical romances use history as a backdrop to place her characters in extraordinary circumstances, where their intense desire for one another grows into the treasured gift of love.

She is the author of Regency and Medieval romance, including: Dukes of Distinction; Soldiers & Soulmates; The St. Clairs; The King's Cousins; and The Knights of Honor.

A native Texan, Alexa lives with her husband in a Dallas suburb, where she eats her fair share of dark chocolate and plots out stories while she walks every morning. She enjoys a good Netflix binge; travel; seafood; and can't get enough of *Survivor* or *The Crown*.

Printed in Great Britain
by Amazon

10711219R00041